summer

Silver City Anthology

Summer 2023

Contents

Dear Readers,
In the atmosphere of video reels, memes, and text messaging, the concept of a printed publication is definitely old-fashioned and arguably out-dated. Having a poem or story, on real paper, in a real book, feels like a thrilling proposition– romantic, the stuff of dreams.

We developed this idea while having coffee on Erica's back porch overlooking Bear Mountain. We are astounded by the support we have received in creating and distributing this humble publication. Many talented writers sent thoughtful submissions, and we are grateful the community has so willingly embraced the idea of an anthology.

We offer you Silver City Anthology, Summer 2023, full of local voices that deserve to have the time and space that the printed page allows. We share with you this bounty of our high-desert community, and hope it brings you as much enjoyment as it has us.

Locally, we have decided to ask only for donations for the first edition, in hopes that it will reach more readers, but anyone anywhere will be able to purchase the anthology on Amazon.

Editor's picks: During the selection process, we each had "favorites" that resonated deeply or moved us, and like a "staff picks" at the antiquated video store, here are some of our favorites from this edition:

Driving by Ralph Bakshi
Reading Blood by Serene Vannoy
The Horologist by Xavi Beltrán

Thank you, again, for being a part of this creative project, even if only for a page or two. We appreciate you sharing this grass-roots magic with us.

With gratitude,
Shanon, Emily, and Erica
silvercityanthology@gmail.com

DRIVING

Ralph Bakshi

so im driving
in the small hours of night
alone
just cruising
and smoking
blue hazy smoke
drifting up
curling around the reasons
why im here
depressed lonely
living alone
hung over
worried about
a crazy girlfriend
driving moves me
through strange
urban landscapes
in los angeles
ventura blvd
burbank
sunland
downtown la
skid row
little tokyo
what's important
in all this gloom
is to have a good car
strong engine

a good radio for late night jazz
coming from some strange
lonely place
that's key
a car that responds well
to my touch
so im not distracted
not worried about breaking down
in this dreary dream
with plenty of cigarettes
i glide past empty storage yards
railroad tracks
lonely downtown streets
with shadows crawling about
closed mexican
and skid row bars
ugly empty glass office buildings
hovering over me as i drive
through highway under passes
into twisting long black boulevards
with weak reflecting lights
on oily slick surfaces
while traffic lights
red yellow green
still blink for me
i glide right through
everything is strange and
then again not
like a philip dick novel
its the same in every city

where i have lived alone
neon reflected emptiness
of a profound level
somehow mixed
with the smoke
jazz and the smooth
low rumble of the car engine
seems to be the absolute truth
that im close to figuring out
as i go over and over
in my mind
how i got here
and what it means
i'm getting close to the answer
i feel it
the sky streaks with light
then coffee in a diner
the truth evaporating
like the smoke in my car

Magnolia Memory

Shelly Barnett

Afternoon hours
spent lying
underneath the fragrant canopy
of creamy saucers
kissing sky.

I could pluck
only a few blossoms
within my reach,
hoping Nana wouldn't notice
they were gone.

Petals became doll fashions—
hats, parasols,
bodices of dresses
attached to skirts of leaves.

Pods, tiny chenille cones
became fruit or desserts
on plates of bark.
Fancy tea parties lasting until dinnertime.

Fondest memories
of placing velvety petals
on my face,
pressing to the shape
of my cheeks,
my forehead,
my closed eyelids.

My mother's touch imagined.

The Horologist

Xavi Beltrán

Through a greasy eye-loupe with a perfect lens that needed cleaning thrice per hour, the horologist made note that the wristwatch before him had a movement with sixteen jewel bearings the color of pigeon blood, which meant they were proper rubies, and one crudely-formed bearing that was the color of bee honey — a topaz — that he knew could have only been fashioned by his own hand during the War, so long ago that his memory began turning backward through time, even as the hands of the wristwatch ticked forward.

Ruby jewel bearings were no larger than mustard seeds, but they were hoarded and restricted during the War, when they were put to good use in gyroscopes, galvanometers, chronometers, and compasses, and in those days the watchmakers on Calle de la Palma had to salvage bearings from other watches, or go without.

But he was no ordinary "watchmaker", he was an horologist — practically a scientist — a mechanical engineer of the tiniest devices, with severe myopia and hands that were steadier than churches built by Spanish stonemasons. Topaz was an inferior gem that was never used for watch bearings, but the horologist had experimented with it almost a lifetime ago, using the most minuscule of machine tools to fashion crude, toroidal specks of topaz that could suffice if placed in the least critical positions. It had been his own trade secret during the War, and to his knowledge, none of the "watchmakers" on Calle de la Palma had ever caught-on.

So: he must have serviced this very timepiece before, many decades ago. But when, and whose was it? The timid boy who presented it seemed barely twenty years of age, asking to sell it, but the watch was of low-quality gold and from a poorly-known maker, so its only appeal in the 21st century would be as a family heirloom, or a piece of nostalgia. Everyone had digital timepieces now, and the detestable mobile phone was now the reason that wristwatches were mostly utilized only for style.

But his client's simple dress and demeanor were neither stylish nor those of a thief, so the horologist agreed to inspect the watch before offering a price, which would not be high, but all old watches can be useful for their parts. The leather wristband was extremely stiff, indicating that the watch had not been worn for a very long time. Perhaps the youth carried it in his pocket as some people do — but there was another thing that was amiss: it raced fast, exceedingly fast, which could only mean that the hairspring had been magnetized. The horologist knew he would have never gone through the trouble of creating a new bearing for a watch that ran so poorly, so he deduced it had been stored in an environment that had magnetized it over time, which might have taken a very long time, indeed.

Through the greasy eye-loupe he glanced at the casing back, a dull golden disk that had already been removed and lay on the workbench next to the watch. It had been engraved in a cursive script by hand; the word TOPO, which was Spanish for "mole" — and then the horologist began to remember the man... the letters were his initials. Was his name Teodoro? No, wait — Teófilo. A señor Teófilo

Parraverde, a professional baker of bread — then a clouded image of the man resurfaced in his mind. A man with green eyes, Teófilo Oscar Parraverde... the second surname might have been Obregón, from his mother's side, but the young client who brought the watch wasn't named Parraverde.

The horologist reached for the ticket and through the eye-loupe observed the thick, tarry streaks of handwriting magnified like tire marks, "José Esposito," and nothing more. It wasn't a common surname in Spanish, but neither was Parraverde, and as the horologist returned to his inspection of the movement, he mulled over the evidence he had.

Teófilo Parraverde had been one of the bakers at La Vasconia, one of the oldest bakeries in Mexico City, situated just on the corner of calles de la Palma and Tacuba. They made not only bread, but cakes and pastries of every kind, flavor, and dimension. If the horologist's memory was correct, this watch would have been perpetually surrounded by sugar and flour, and as he gently pried the mica crystal away from the bezel, he confirmed the presence of an ancient, particulate grime that matched his expectations. It would be a miracle if Teófilo were still kneading the dough today, but the old wristwatch with its engraving had definitely belonged to that man, and this demanded a casual inquiry even if the youth was not a thief.

The horologist reached for the detestable mobile phone: of course he had no choice but to own one himself, for placing and receiving calls, and he could not deny that it was handy for setting any mechanical watch to the correct time, and measuring their speed. His ironic dependence on the superior enemy was a source of frustration that smoldered in his mind like an ember, but it also kept him in touch with his clients, as rotary dial-phones were perfectly capable of doing. But things had changed, and it's true that rotary phones can't tell time.

— Panadería Vasconia, hello. Does a mister Parraverde still work over there?

— La Señora Parraverde? Jacinta, you mean?

— Yes — said the horologist, which really meant "No, but now I understand".

— She's not here at the moment, she leaves every day at 5:00.

— By the bells? — asked the horologist, referring to the Metropolitan cathedral tower.

— Yes indeed, how do you know? Are you a friend?

— I'm only now just getting to know her. Thank you, and goodbye.

———

Watchmakers don't really "make" watches. They buy, they sell, they repair, they adjust. Their task is not to create things, but to correct them, while keeping their techniques mysterious from the masses. They can detect the subtlest deviations that would escape the common eye, even as their own eyes fail to see anything larger than the lens of a loupe. They determine the source of an exquisite problem both by examining each component, and by assessing the whole machine. It takes many years of experience to comprehend the complexity of how the pieces integrate — the escape wheel, the tourbillion, the regulator, the balance gear, the pinions, the jumper, the pallet fork, and the ratchet — It's said that the most complex watch ever made had more than 1700 parts, and yet the story of the Parraverde family was so much simpler than that.

When the youth José returned the next morning, looking equally hopeful and hopeless, the horologist said to him:

"The watch isn't worth very much, but it can be fixed to run quite well. I recommend that you keep it. Do you have a mobile phone?"

"No I don't", said José — which the horologist already knew, but thought courteous to ask.

"If it's money that you need, they are always looking for notaries at Santo Domingo."

"What is a notary?"

"It's a literate person who writes proper documents and signs them, for people who cannot. And you will need this watch to record the times that you provide your signature. You can read and write proper Spanish, can't you?"

"I think so," said José.

"Then go to plaza Santo Domingo with my recommendation. Give anyone my card. Find some work as a notary, learn what you can today, and come back for your wristwatch at 5."

"How will I know when it's 5, if I leave the watch with you?"

"By the bells of the cathedral," said the horologist softly, as he bowed his head to continue his work through the loupe.

And the myopic old horologist never saw nor needed to know that José's eyes were also green, like his grandfather's had been, but neither did he need to know the thickness of the escapement in order to calibrate it, or the number of coils on any watchspring, or that it had been an iron safe box at the convent orphanage that had magnetized the watch after 18 years of storage. The horologist had assumed it was kept in something like that by the Italian nuns who accepted the infant, along with the only item of value his desperate mother could offer up — a very plain gold watch that had belonged to her father, that might somehow pay the child's expenses or be sold upon his release. The Italian nuns had schooled him well and named him "Esposito" or "the exposed", a name that is given to many foundlings and orphans, and while the horologist had assembled all of this from the clues, he didn't need to confirm whether Jacinta was really the young man's mother, because Parraverde is such an unusual last name, and if Jacinta told time by the cathedral bells it meant that she was either poor, or old, or both. The fact the bakery had asked with interest whether the horologist was her friend confirmed the fact that she was a woman alone in the world, with neither a husband nor a son, just as José was also alone in the world and had been even more alone since his apparent emancipation.

The horologist fixed the watch and did not ask José to pay, but no mechanical watch is without its own peculiar rhythm. Each lever and gear will mesh at its own time, and so the horologist would neither force the hands forward nor back, but only optimize the mechanism and wind up the spring. The rest would unfold on its own.

La Vasconia was situated directly between Calle la Palma and Santo Domingo, where José did find a bit of work, and once the horologist learned that he left work at 5:00 — by the clock and not the bells, which always rang late — it took only a small adjustment to the watch to ensure that José would eventually, sooner or later, be standing right in front of La Vasconia just as his mother might be leaving, or might even enter to buy bread, not precisely at 5:00, but that wasn't important, and it was only a matter of time before she would recognize the green eyes and her own father's watch.

A timepiece can keep track of events, but it can also incite them, and this time it was because the horologist, who was no ordinary watchmaker, deliberately tuned a mediocre wristwatch to run 4 minutes slow by the end of the day. When there are sixteen ruby bearings, each one smaller than a mustard seed, having the last one made of topaz works just fine if you know where to place it.

And as I drove, gasping and stuttering my now tiny yawps, I dug in the passenger seat for the burrito bought at breakfast that I knew I wouldn't eat then but would need later - perfect pinto beans and melting cheese and tender steak and that soft flour tortilla and all the weird comfort of it... And I eat it.

I've never known how to give up, give in, and now is not the time to learn.

Beginnings and endings have a cyclical nature, looping back and gliding forward, this closure here, that opening there- we perceive time as linear but my experiences within time swaddle both the past and the future in the present - my life is written in cursive.

I understand that this tangible event marked on the curving limbs of time does not make determinations of what will come. It's a point on a line, made to branch off of.

I have work to do when I get home.

Catching Lizards
Natalee Drissell

Step 1: Scan the local surfaces. Be inquisitive, steady; use your eyes like microscopes.

Step 2: Overcast skies slow their movements; watch the weather like a TV weatherman.

Step 3: Once you've spotted a scaly back or tail, move quickly; make your hands move like lizards themselves.

Step 4: Corral your prey; guide them with your movements, cup your hands over the spot you saw them last.

Step 5: Stroke their smooth soft skin. Be surprised by its warm aliveness, and more surprised by the depth mere seconds hold.

Step 6: Remember you are the predator; respect one moment as enough, and let them escape.

Jealous January

Savvy Egge

The grass is always greener

But Autumn's grass is dead?

Oh April's blooms and open rooms

They must be had instead.

December's frosty air

Is surely to be envied

But what to wear?

That brand new pair

Of summer shoes,

She's friendly.

All I have is New Year's Eve

And made up resolutions

January, who am I?

In need of substitutions?

Becoming Nobody

Gabe Eyrich

“He who delights in solitude is either a wild beast or a god.” - Friedrich Nietzsche

Friday, June 21 - afternoon
Trimming the rosemary
Is it dying?
Why?
Thinning the corn plants
Mulching the flower beds
I am in the sun too long without cover
Watering the gardens
The apricot tree is dying, too
Dryness?

Saturday, June 22 – morning
How quickly we become like animals in the heat
pausing under shade trees

The fire smoke is a blanket
under which cicadas’ songs are amplified
making the morning landscape turn a shade of blue
to match the sky
Smoke collects in the throat

Sunday, June 23 - morning
When baby Coyote found the brown hair tie outside
I asked his mom if it was hers
She didn’t know
But why leave it on the sidewalk?
I wear it on my wrist now
Noticing it as I push the sleeves of my shirt down to
protect my skin from sun

I have lupus
I am a scavenger

How much can I reconstruct from memory?

Avery texts as I approach the base of the hill
She is traveling by plane to the west coast for a therapeutic wilderness adventure
She writes in jest: If you wanna feel VERY smug and superior, wear your new form fitted merino wool mid weight zipper pullover by REI and take your own travel mug and water bottle.

How can I hate the privileged now? The Patagonia wearers, fancy-tent campers, high-tech gear collectors, cross-country fliers? Because I love Avery.

I look down at my dirty feet in six-year-old Chacos, my yellow thrift shop pants and oversized button down. My hair is uncombed, wild, my sunhat a faded salmon, my sunglasses clouded from sweat and dust. I carry a worn black leash, an iPhone, am tangled in headphones and the leather rope which keeps my hat attached to me. What a mess. I am superior to no one. I walk here in constancy, in smallness, in relative poverty. And the whole world (it sometimes seems) is moving quickly, erratically, and here I remain, still.

Friday, June 22 - evening
Sasha finds us
She moves her whole, dusty, shedding body against my clean yellow pants

I laugh
I love her – black German Shepherd with paws nearly as big as my hands
Her ears give her trouble so I try not to touch them
I kiss her nose
She sniffs me and licks my face,
Collapses in the dirt for a belly rub
My own dog comes and goes
They do not compete

I trade in Vivaldi for vintage Mary J Blige
Ascending the hill, I see a man
The sun is setting in the west and blinding him slightly
I explain that the German Shepherd is friendly
I think he cannot hear me – headphones? And he is shielding his eyes from the sun. But he gets it when we are closer. He has brown skin with many tattoos, wears a white tank, wishes me a good evening, and I him.

Tuesday, June 18 - afternoon

My mornings (and evenings) are spent walking in the open spaces near home with my dog. Today, the academic requirement that I finish Aldo Leopold's, *A Sand County Almanac*, means looping through the same territory over and over while listening to the book's narration on Audible. I take notes on my phone as I walk.

If everything in the land body has a purpose, like the wolf or the juniper, then what is ours - our human purpose - collectively, as a species? Leopold dichotomizes between the land body and the human body, yet he also speaks of ecology and the relationships of all things in the context of a system.

For instance, of what use is it that humans go into nature to excavate our own psyches? We do it. We are unique in our ability to do it. How does that contribute to the ecological whole?

Leopold also says that, "Man kills what he loves," and that, "An ecologist lives alone in a world of wounds."

Wednesday, June 19 - evening
My mother's birthday
Joy Harjo becomes the first Native American Poet Laureate
Ta-Nehisi Coates testifies before congress about reparations
Refugees flood Deming and are welcomed
Thirsty deer come into the neighborhood at midday looking for water

I listen to Joy Harjo's "Fear Poem" accompanied by drums as I walk
I sob uncontrollably

"…I am not afraid to be angry
I am not afraid to rejoice
I am not afraid to be hungry
I am not afraid to be full
I am not afraid to be black
I am not afraid to be white
I am not afraid to be hated
I am not afraid to be loved…"

Monday, June 17 - evening
Happiness Frequency Serotonin Release Music

Vivaldi Concerto for 2 Cellos, String Orchestra and Continuo in G Minor, RV 531: 1. Allegro performed by Bobby McFerrin and the Saint Paul Chamber Orchestra, "Paper Music"
When I listen to this music on the evening walk, I conduct
This music and the movements required of the tongue to produce it are deeply sensual
Nature, too, is deeply sensual
I am with Eros tonight

Friday, June 14 – afternoon
The goal of my writing is to explore the movement between an identity-less self in nature and an identity-full self in the social world.

The goal of the writing is to explore duality and singularity.
The goal is to explore how the commodification of nature by those with social privilege is damaging, how it reinforces the otherness of nature rather than unifying human and nature, the latter which is, ironically, often the spoken intention.

[Reflection: I am not sure that I care, not when I am in nature, with nature, in communion.]

Day Unknown - morning
Listening

Symphony of cicadas
Surround sound

Dog panting
Heavy breathing
Tongue out

Dripping

Cars in the distance
Tires over pavement

Dog panting

A truck now
A bark

Crescendo

Standing in the shade of juniper
Dirt and rock underfoot

Stones with green and chartreuse paintings
yellow
silent

Standing in the shade

A car horn
Barking in the distance
Cicadas

No dog panting

Juniper
Mesquite
Cat's claw
Yucca

All parched
I am parched

Blue sky
White wisps
A power line
A fence

Moving

My dog
A grasshopper

The sound of human feet
Navigating a rocky slope
A hill with a penchant for throwing me down

A fly
A song bird's cry

My feet slip
Dog in the marsh now
Dappled shade

Morning dove
song bird
cicada
In conversation

Maybe the cars, too
My feet
Sliding rocks
Crunching leaves

There is honeysuckle
But no ravens

A low hanging juniper branch
catches my hair
Silver leaves rustle

It is greener here by the water

I turn my human music on
Black artists, rhythmic

There are no black people in this wilderness

Only white
Some brown

My hair is pale like the dry grass
Like the seeds of the purple thistle after blooming

My animal, as black and sleek as the ravens
Which are not here

Magenta cholla fruit
A spark of color

A blooming bird of paradise
Red yellow
green

Here the skeleton of a tree like an old man whose limbs have buckled and bent
Maybe he walks with a cane
Maybe most of his teeth are gone
And the skin on his cheeks is collapsing inward
The joints in his hands are swollen
Bulging knuckles
Translucent skin
Veins
That is what the tree looks like

And the mullein
My favorite soft plant
At once so female at its center
Until it blooms into a male
And then back again
I drink rain drops from it with my own tongue
When there is rain

Dog panting
We move along

Buzzing insects
Cicadas
A truck rumbling

Broken glass
Hooked burs

Flags in the distance:
USA
New Mexico
Prisoner of War

Someone's made a peace sign in the dirt with stones

We cross a road
Cross back over the wasteland

Another planet

Tires
Chunks of concrete
Rusted pipes
PVC
Remnants of a garbage container

Someone has made a stone path
Someone else has taken parts of it away

The cicadas continue
A truck
A breeze through my hair
the sound of hollowness
Dogs barking
Flags clanking against a metal pole
A grasshopper

My dog waits in the shade

For me to leash us
And continue home
Through the streets

Wild
Not wild
We two

But smiling

Sunday, June 23 - evening

Dear Class,

I am finding that between phenomenological exercises and reading Aldo Leopold that I have lost my own (familiar) writer's voice, and seemingly, some cognitive ability. My brain is not thinking in complete sentences. It is sometimes thinking in images, possibly in sensations, if it is thinking at all. True, this could be a result not of the course material but of time spent in the sun, inciting a lupus flare which casts a low fog in my brain. In the past weeks, I have walked almost from Silver City to Las Cruces (nearly one hundred miles!), but here, in the open spaces outside my door, with my dog, Sanjay. We are taking a break this evening. I speak this gently to him. He is disappointed, likely still hoping, and resting by my side.

But, isn't it also possible that the walking in total presence with the land body for so many mornings and evenings could impact the way one's mind works? Could I be thinking like a mountain? Or a . . .
.

White feather, soft, floating above tall grasses on the hillside in the morning sun

I do not see many people. It is a life of relative ascetism that I live: Me, my animals, the land, an adobe cell, simple foods, tea.
I want to tell you that it is difficult to be a wilderness guide in the desert who has an adversarial relationship with the sun. My body's immune system will attack itself if given too much light, limiting its own mobility and covering its skin with a rash.

Saturday, June 22 - morning
Breeze, cool from the west
A pine tree
Trucks in the distance
The sound of wind

A shadow
Half of a waning moon at 9:00 AM
Up high
Against a blue sky

Black dog running up hill
My pants flagging in the wind
Sun beating on the back of my neck

The truck sound is coming from the cemetery
Digging a grave
Amongst the white crosses and silk flowers of Catholicism

Dogs from the animal shelter bark in concert
Enjoying their morning exercise

We walk on
My nose bleeding slightly from the dryness
Always I am asking the pine trees for help

Here a bridge
Three bridges

A family of quail
My dog knows he will not catch
So he listens, panting

Beneath the umbrella of deciduous trees in summer
Fanning us cool
Verdant against the sky

We walk on

Into the dry wash
Over a concrete embankment
Marked by translucent spider webs

Through the pines now
Over a carpet of brown needles

The wind stills
Crickets

We walk on

Broken and twisted trees
Long dead
But beautiful

My hair lifts slightly in the breeze
A bird calls

Another now, but sweeter
A soprano
Harmonizing with a buzzing alto

Tree roots
Rock dams
White open poppies in the sunlight
A plastic bottle full of sand

We walk on

Power lines and water tanks
A shelter for abused women and children
A wall
A security code
Dark slate rock underfoot, breaking

Dried grasses in circular patterns
Footprints
Spikes of cactus
Low to the ground

How do animals know to avoid them?

Tree roots strong enough now to support my body
Shade between junipers

Billowing pants, hair lifting

Shh....

The birds

Sidewalks
Yellow lines on a curving road

Where is my dog?
I hear human voices from the women's shelter, a laugh

I walk on
I hear his tags following me, his panting
His toenails against concrete
His spit making water marks beneath him

Butterflies the size of my pinky finger
A copper mine in the distance

We walk on
ATV tracks in the dirt
Eroded hillside
Will it hold?

Silver rabbitbrush
The sound of my own feet
Over the same wasteland
With the same flags

A town unfolds

And a crow!
Before me in the tree
Talking
As a second alights

So good to see you!
Where have you been?
What does this dryness do to our psyches?

Monday, June 24 - morning

Body tired
Joints, ankles, knees stiff
Muscles sore
Exposed flesh throbbing

I sit in the shade
Sanjay comes

Our bond is deeper for these walks in the wilderness

His body is lithe, well-muscled strong
He does not have lupus or take medications
Two cups of food per day at regular intervals
And lots of rabbit chasing

Sometimes he wins
Evidence that the chase matters

Cicadas in waves
Persistent crickets
And a motorcycle engine

A car alarm
And a hole in the dirt
Whose home?

Crossing over barbed wire and the remnants of a box spring
Electrical pole 4113
My legs like molasses

It is never tiresome descending to the place where water is, but isn't
The green betrays the hidden, subterranean

moisture
There is a cool freshness, a lightening of spirit

But we are just passing through
A constant bird calling

February '96 – Montana

Dawn Falch

Longing for Spring, rebirth

days getting deceptively warmer

glimmers of hope

trick me into thinking

there could be a thaw

yet I am frozen as the ground.

The sun, warm on my face

shines through

glass covered with frost

feathery patterns

of crystalline cold

bitter reminders

that Winter remains

lingering on the Earth

and in my heart.

Untitled

Feral Farm Girl

Her life was as delicate as a dandelion.
One little puff, from any direction,
And it was completely shattered.
But that was the beauty of it.
For each seed contained a bit of her magick,
And was spread across the world,
Blessing all who touched it.
And, like the dandelion, she simply
Regrew herself.
Spreading joy and nectar to the bees
And to anyone humble enough to
Appreciate her beauty and sacrifice.

Coffee Mugs

EG Fritz

It was the coffee mugs that finally made me cry. There were just so many of them.

I had loaded the dishwasher in the late afternoon. Was it only yesterday? School had dismissed, but he was still at work, and I was already thinking of dinner preparations. Then, the phone rang. It was one of his colleagues. He had suddenly become ill... had collapsed... had some kind of episode... and was taken to the hospital. I grabbed keys and was out the door.

Mugs had come to us in small batches around holidays, and at the end of each term. Most came from the dollar store or Walmart. Some were filled with sweets or accompanied by a small stuffed toy. They had cards attached bearing sentiments like "To the Best Teacher!" and "Thank you for helping me learn". I was always happy for him, and very proud of these expressions of respect and affection from his students. He shared the sweets with me and put the stuffed toys on a shelf in his home office, squeezed in between the books, binders, notepads, and pencil caddies. The coffee mugs went to the kitchen cupboard for daily use. I appreciated them as practical, tangible, rewards for the time, effort, and emotional energy that he invested in his job, in his students.

I don't remember the drive to the hospital, other than the effort I made to stay within the speed limit, and the fear that sat like a boulder in my gut. Then, somehow, I was there, being shown into the exam room where he lay quietly on a gurney.

As time passed and the cupboard shelves slowly filled with more mugs, I started to feel a little irritated. Couldn't they think up a new kind of gift? I couldn't remember which mugs were actual gifts from students, and which few were anonymous exchange gifts from staff and faculty holiday parties. Although I expected him to feel a little sentimental, I assumed that he had also lost track of the names and faces of the givers. Seriously, who could remember? How many mugs could one teacher use? The trouble was that he did use them. Not only were the shelves full, but the dishwasher always had several gifted mugs in each load. And the "pretty" mugs that matched our plates? Seldom used. It offended my sense of... I don't know... how things should be...?

I held his hand, while they asked questions. Had he ever had this or that condition? What was his family background? Was I alright to go home alone? Could they help me in any way? Dazed, I answered as best as I could.

While he always chose one of his mugs, I served him coffee in the "pretty" mugs, whenever I had a chance. I also mentioned the full cupboard once or twice, but he hated getting rid of anything. Finally, during a spring-cleaning spree, I took all of the gifted mugs out of the cupboard and placed them on the counter. I asked him to help me sort out which, if any, could be given to the local thrift shop, to relieve the crowded shelves. Reluctantly, he looked them over and searched his memory, slowly picking out two or three that he couldn't attach a name or face to. I quickly whisked those away to a box for donations. Whew! I felt progress had been made. I thought, in a few months, maybe we can cull a few more.

Then, he began to pick up the other mugs, one by one, and to tell me stories about each student who had honored him with their humble gift. There was Marlene, who no one knew needed glasses, until he noticed her straining to see his notes on the board. And Omar, with a learning disability, undiagnosed until his teacher brought certain behaviors to the attention of the school psychologist. And years later, the graduations where they asked him to pose with them for photos. While I saw a mug covered with dead presidents, he saw Paloma, who remembered his love of history, and brought a souvenir from her special field trip to Washington DC. The generic holiday mug that said "Ho, ho, ho!" became Alex. And of course, the Santa mugs were Debbie and Sophia, the giggly, yet studious duo who liked to hang out in the classroom after school to straighten books and sort papers. The motorcycle mug was Joaquin, and the one with the U.S. flag was Destiny. For him, the mugs took on the personalities of the givers.

I stroked his cool brow as they told me what had happened, and stated their diagnosis.

The memories didn't stop with those who gave gifts. He recalled their friends and classmates, many whose dads were not around, and who needed him, not only as a teacher, but as a positive male role model. The memories also branched out to the families of his students. As a result of his efforts, Marlene's mother, who had been struggling to find work and to learn English, was put in touch with a community adult education program, and was hired as an assistant in the school library. There were two girls whose mom, "the cake lady", always baked for class birthday parties. Remember when their big brother became an intern to a US Congresswoman, and later was elected to the school board? The time when Anisa joyfully told him she had been diagnosed with PTSD. She wasn't crazy! What she had was really "a thing"! When Destiny returned from a family vacation a rip tide. There were Monique and Tina, who constantly misbehaved, but who made a beautiful farewell poster for him when he left to teach at another school. There was Roman, a tough kid who talked back and resisted learning with everything in him, yet excitedly jumped up out of his seat to greet "Mr!" when his teacher showed up to fill in for a different class. Yes, there were quite a few mugs, but so very many more memories!

I caressed the salt and pepper stubble of his pale cheek, as they discussed the actions that needed to be taken.

His nostalgic smile and the soft, far-away look in his eyes completely dispelled my negative feelings. Every one of those mugs served up a warm helping of recollections with his morning coffee. With a renewed sense of gratitude, I put the mugs away, realizing that the kitchen cupboard was much more than just a practical storage area. It had become a sacred place, a kind of magic portal to a time and place full of tears and smiles, trials and triumphs, and of watching his students learn and grow. Those mugs formed the background for a significant chapter of his life story.

The hard lump of fear in my belly gradually softened and spread until it surrounded me like a shroud.

Needless to say, the precious memory mugs

continued to be used regularly, and the "pretty" mugs stayed on the shelf, untouched, for the most part. The only difference was in my perspective. I had come to understand that he actually did remember the giver of each and every mug, and that those memories helped him stay connected to the positive aspects of a very demanding profession. He kept those memories alive, and kept working long hours, late nights, and weekends, striving to do his best for his students. He also kept sharing their stories and his hopes for them with me, while he drank his morning brew from any one of his special mugs. Life went on.

I was lost in a fog, but somehow able to keep moving. They said "go home and rest, for now".

I drove home through the darkness, and somehow accomplished my nighttime routine. I fed the dogs, and locked up the house for the night, but my thoughts were still with him. Exhausted in every way, I finally slept, waking once or twice, only to quickly close my eyes at the memory of the hospital room, his hair fanned out on the crisp white pillowcase, his face, peaceful, but so pale.

This morning, I still moved around as if drugged, slow and unsure. My routine was full of holes. The things I regularly did out of love, out of a desire to lighten his load didn't need doing. There was no breakfast to prepare for him, only my bowl of cereal. No lunch to pack for him to take to work. No need to make sure he had his phone, school keys, and backpack full of textbooks and graded papers. I did my best to skip past the missing parts of the morning, feeling my way, a fragmented soul lacking enough light to see through the darkness.

I searched for things I could do to keep moving, all the while talking to myself. *Life is about change*... I fed the dogs and let them out to run. *Some changes are bigger and scarier than others*... I grabbed a broom to sweep the little porch. *Try to think positively*... Resolutely, I returned to the kitchen and started to unload the dishwasher. *No more lesson planning weekends*... First put away the plates and bowls. *No more parent conference evenings*... then the silverware goes into the drawer. *Just keep moving*... Pulling out the top rack, I put away drinking glasses. *No more grading papers late at night...* Lastly, I reached for his coffee mugs. Lifting the first one, I was struck by the fact that I was holding one of his treasures and I closed my eyes. *There would be no more students with their gifts*... For a moment, I felt as though he had left that hospital bed and was there with me. *Memories will live on*... Slowly, lovingly, I placed each mug on the shelf remembering the all-night grading sessions, the exhaustion he felt so much of the time. *He could rest now*... The stories he frequently shared with me about the students who needed extra help, the ones that made him laugh, and sadly, the troubled ones, those that had he felt unable to reach. *The hard work was finished*... The memories from those years washed over me. With one hand on the cupboard door, and the other still lingering on the final shelved mug, I stood for some time, tasting salty tears, clinging to my memories of the strong man he had been, drawing strength for the days ahead. *Life is about change*... Slowly, reluctantly, I closed the door, leaving the mugs in the cool, sacred darkness of the cupboard. All the memories, his and mine, I tucked away in my aching heart.

Healing

Tom Hester

Months before the vacation west to New Mexico, Allie Garrett had given up moaning when pain tore her belly as though with tongs. Instead, she whimpered lightly and sucked in air in sharp, sibilant breaths.

Hank glanced at the rear-view mirror. A cloud of dust boiled up from the rutted road, and through the van's rear window the world became a receding tunnel of swirling dirt. His daughter Allie, whom he called Sparky, lay on her side. Her head lolled on the seat, and her dark eyes were like targets, circled outside by dark lines and inside by pink.

Allie's twin Pike, a hulking sixteen-year old, hunched next to her, staring into the cholla and yucca that stretched in tangles from the road to the horizon. Pike's ear buds, buzzing with indie rock, accounted for his empty stare, although Hank knew that his son had heard Allie's whimpers and now tried to avert both ears and eyes.

Mary, the eight-year old, slept on the back seat. She resembled a trout snoring on a floor of a large aquarium. If she had been awake, her father could have seen the distress at her older sister's attack, distress that Pike felt but did not show. Hank understood that it often took two of his children to display a complete emotion.

Rather than focusing on control of the bucking vehicle, Hank sorted memories of Allie's illness. What was it that her doctor at Johns Hopkins had said? Hank ran through his mental list of big medical words. Idiopathic expression of essential endometriosis? The terms had no authentic meaning for Hank and his wife Barbara, but as the first diagnosis without tentative edges, they were relieved to have it.

The doctor had a broad Russian face and hands appropriate for a woodworker or sculptor. Her fingers, though not long, looked powerful. Hank remembered thinking that maybe she performed esoteric Ukranian finger exercises. She was calm, very efficient, and unlike the physicians consulted earlier, looked into their eyes as much as she looked at the lab results. And she was not apologetic about the diagnosis. As Barbara had said to Hank the evening after they had gotten the news, "She seemed pretty comfortable with Allie having the condition." Hank knew what Barbara meant. The doctor pitied neither Allie nor them.

The van veered on a washboarded section where the sand had given way to rock. The rear yawed toward the front and Hank felt the tires skip. An airborne van at 15 miles an hour. Barbara, in her copilot mode, staring down the road to will away rocks and craters, shot him a look.

“How much farther?" Barbara said.

Hank looked at the odometer. "We've done seven miles so far. Could be any time now. Your sister wasn't too definite about the mileage, you know."

Barbara nodded. She and Hank agreed on Starry. Starry wasn't her real name. Margaret was. But she had adopted "Starry" when she moved to an alternative community outside Silver City. At home in Virginia among their friends, Barbara and Hank referred to her as Starry Holistic, in honor of her work as a vitamin therapist practicing with a consortium of Anglo women who asserted ties to either Hindu mystics or American Indian medicine workers.

"When she was describing the house, I had the impression that there would be plenty of shacks along the road. So far, nothing." Barbara turned her face into the sunlight that glinted past the windshield. Her tinted glasses gave her an almost Hollywood air. Barbara had a chiseled jaw and high cheek bones.

"Nothing" hung in the air of the van. The wheels hit a ditch dug at an angle across the road. Passengers and detritus from the weeklong trip leaped and settled. Allie groaned.

"Sorry, Sparky, we're almost there now. Hold on. Aunt Starry said that we'll find the curing woman soon." In the mirror Hank saw Allie bury her face into the upholstery.

Late in the night, whispering in intense syllables, Starry had spoken of the Mexican curing woman. "You will never forgive yourselves if you don't find Maria Vasconcelos and have her place her hands on Allie." Starry, Hank and Barbara were sitting at the tiny table in Starry's cramped kitchen, which had the feeling of a nineteenth century apothecary shop. On narrow shelves stood quart Mason jars filled with dried mushrooms, raw nuts, leaves, seeds, and twigs that have never been pictured on a food label. The shelves rose in ranks from floor to ceiling on the wall next to the three-burner stove. A half-dozen types of rice were arrayed in burlap sacks along the back of the only counter.

Allie had arrived at Starry's house in obvious agony, possibly aggravated by the long days on the interstate. The three medicines that the Johns Hopkins team had prescribed had had little effect.

"Probably hormones that will wind up killing her," Starry said. Barbara objected. Starry had no right to criticize them when they were doing the best they could.

"You told me yourself that they don't know why she has this pain," Starry said. Barbara admitted that, and her eyes filled with tears. Hank felt her anger and frustration and shared her defensiveness.

In round cursive letters, Starry had written directions to Maria's house. Starry was a little fuzzy about the spelling of the whole name so she placed a big "V" after "Maria." Hank had the legal pad sheet on top the driver's console. "7-8 MI" it said. "Little white adobe house on left. Old car in front yard." How many houses could that describe? Hank wondered.

The road curved and at the point where it again turned east stood a white-washed adobe. A Plymouth Valiant, battered and rusting and minus its tires, slumped next to what appeared to be a pen of chicken wire. A large black dog panted under a privet bush. Two children in clothes almost the color of the ground were crouched at the outside corner of the house.

Hank stopped the van in the road. The older of the two children stood. She was a girl of about seven or eight, Mary's age. Her face had a serious expression, and as soon as Hank edged the van into the yard, she ran as instant as a ghost into the house, leaving the door open. Hank steered the van over a berm separating the road from the front yard. The yard looked smoother than the road.

By the time the Garrett family had unfurled from the van, a woman appeared at the door. She stood no more than five feet tall, and her bare arms were like thick, dried vines. She wore a black dress swathed and cinched around her frame. The dress hem brushed the floor, gathering a rim of dust.

"Maria?" Barbara asked, walking toward the woman.

The woman smiled. Her few teeth jutted this way and that in her mouth, but the smile was welcoming, not automatic. "Si. Si," the woman said in a throaty voice. "Pasenles. Pasen, por favor." She held out her skinny arms. Behind her, peering toward the newcomers who were gathered in front of the concrete blocks that served as steps, stood the girl. Hank looked for the little boy whom he had seen from the road, but the corner play area, where evidently some four-year-old excavation was going on, was empty. The boy and the dog had disappeared.

Hank then squinted at the late morning sky which was silver at the edges and a sober blue at the crown despite the sun bleaching the very air. A hot wind moved across the sage and rabbit brush that rimmed the yard, and Hank suddenly felt thirsty.

"Maria," Barbara said. "Our daughter is ill. We were told....My sister Starry told me that you might help her. We would like....We will pay..." Allie had descended from the van and stood next to her mother for a minute or two but then had begun to lean into Barbara. By the time Barbara reached the end of her appeal, Allie was grasping her mother's arm and was bent forward in a bow.

"Pasenles, por favor." The old woman stepped down to one of the blocks and gently gripped Allie's right hand to guide her inside. The old woman was bare footed, and her feet, almost black but with a white alkali crust, looked even older than she.

The room was dark and cool. Beans cooking on the stove filled the house with a dusky scent. A Sylvania television console brooded against the wall next to the door and on top of it was a newer, apparently more capable, portable television. From the kitchen the radio stuttered Spanish.

Not releasing Allie's hand, Maria led the girl toward a high double bed in a sort of alcove carved from the corner of the room. Hank thought that Allie must really be feeling punk if she allowed the old woman to put her on a strange bed. A patchwork quilt covered the bed, and Maria soothed the girl onto the quilt and then spread a knitted red afghan over her. Despite the scorching glare outside, here Allie would need warmth.

Maria caressed the girl's face. Arthritis gnarled her fingers. The skin on her hands was crinkled like cooked parchment.

Barbara spoke. "Ma soeur... Ma fille est malade." It was the wrong foreign language, but it was the only one that Barbara knew. She stepped to the bed and put one hand on Allie's shoulder and the other on Maria's forearm. "Maria, she's very young. Her life has so much promise. And she is sick. Malade. Can you make her well?" Two tears coursed down Barbara's cheeks. She gripped the old woman's hand.

Allie did not turn away, as Hank expected. She lay on her back. Her eyes were closed. She seemed to have fallen into a slumber. She did not whimper.

How long the three adults stood at the side of the bed, Hank later could not recall. He vaguely remembered Maria stroking Allie's frizzy blond hair and saying "purty," which was the only English Hank heard her say.

Pike stood in the middle of the room, scarcely moving. He looked at the Sylvania console, the first such television that he had seen outside pictures and films. The green screen gave him the sense of a faraway land, as though it were a Ming Dynasty lacquer piece or a Mayan altar. If he could twist those substantial bakelite knobs, Pike knew that he could see Carl Reiner and Sid Caesar on *The Show of Shows*.

Pike stepped toward the shrine to the Virgin of Guadalupe, whose picture hung on the wall above a rickety table the size of a stool. Plastic clematis twined over the golden plastic frame around the Virgin and dangled down the wall where three sere crosses woven of reeds were nailed. Candles burned in bottles arranged on a white crocheted doily. An image of the Virgin was stenciled on one bottle's glass, although this Virgin looked less pious to Pike than the one in the picture. Decorating another candle bottle, a black man in a monk's robe raised his right arm in a blessing. The flame of this candle guttered. Wallet size photographs leaned against the candles and were stuck between the Virgin's picture and the frame. Three people in the photos Pike recognized: the little boy (much younger), the little girl (much younger), and the old woman as a middle-aged woman in a print dress holding the hand of a teenage girl.

Two much larger studio photographs, one framed

and one curling and stained, were pinned between the candles and the wall. They showed the same subject, a glamorous Mexican woman in her early twenties. A photographer's invented halo highlighted her silky brown hair. Pike couldn't interpret the glint in her eyes. Was it laughter? Sex? Life? He knew it was something good, for the photographs made him happy.

To one side of the shrine a mayonnaise jar held rolled up sheets of paper and envelopes. Even in the dim Pike could see that these were utility bills. Piled in front of the jar were some dollar bills and quarters.

The radio advertised a dance in a shouted mash of English and Spanish. As though they were ducking under the reverberations, Mary and the Mexican girl sprawled on the plank floor, arranging the dress of a worn doll that lay between them. The girl sprang up from her crouch and went to the sink. She turned on the water and it clattered into an aluminum kettle that she lifted to the stove's front burner. The beans cooked on the back burner. Then she filled two fourteen ounce jelly glasses with water and took them to Hank and Barbara, sloshing the water on the planks.

"Water?" the girl mumbled.

"Thanks," Hank said. He remembered his thirst and took a deep draught. Barbara also smiled her thanks and sipped. The water was cold.

The girl returned to the stove and waited for the kettle's whistle. At its first breath she poured hot water into two colored mugs. She spooned coffee from a Nescafe jar and sugar from a bowl without a lid. Her teaspoon clanged against the glass of the mugs. She carried the two mugs to the metal and Formica table. She retrieved three graham crackers from a wax paper wrap and placed them between the mugs. Both Pike and Mary watched her as they might observe a performer on stage producing feats of balance and magic.

"Want some coffee? Please." the girl said to Hank.

"What?" Hank said, for he had been watching Maria stroking Allie's forehead and neck.

The girl pointed toward the coffee.

"Oh, thanks so much. No. No, I couldn't. The water is perfect." Hank held up his empty jelly glass.

Allie was sitting up in the bed. In the gloom she looked vibrant, as though waking fully rested from a long nap. Anxiety and fear lifted from Hank and Barbara, almost as visible as the steam above the mugs, and a sense of confidence had somehow replaced powerlessness.

"We must go," Barbara said. She stepped from the bed's edge to hug the girl. But the girl remained stiff. Barbara turned toward Maria. “Thank you, Maria. Muchas gracias.” Barbara hugged the old woman.

“Sparky, we’ve got to go.” Hank said.

Allie set aside the red afghan. She swung her feet off the edge of the bed and lightly leaped to the floor. She slipped her feet into her sandals and followed Barbara in hugging Maria.

When the old woman stepped back, Barbara saw that she was weeping, covering her eyes with a handkerchief.

“What’s wrong?” she asked. Understanding that she

would not receive answer from Maria, Barbara turned to the girl. “Why is Maria crying?”

The girl said something rapidly to the old woman who murmured a reply as her open hand hid her eyes.

“Abuelita says that your daughter feels like her own daughter. She remembers.”

“Where is her daughter now?” Barbara asked.

The girl turned toward the shrine, and Hank and Barbara knew that she was looking at the two large portraits.

“She is dead, Senora. When my brother born, she died.”

“Oh, I’m so sorry.” Barbara said.

Hank gathered Mary, Pike and Allie. He shoved his hand into his pocket and fished out several bills that he put on the shrine. Then he moved his children toward the door. When Hank opened the door, the boy was sitting on the concrete blocks. He looked up and almost simultaneously dashed toward the chicken wire pen. The black dog growled and backed away, never turning his back to the four Barretts heading toward their customary seats in the van.

Within a minute, time enough for Hank to start the van, Barbara emerged from the door, which she did not shut. She was crying. She ignored the dog as she strode across the gravel. The way she opened and slammed the passenger side door of the van seemed angry. She looked toward the house as the van circled the yard and just missed the Valiant.

Just after Hank steered the van over the berm into the road, a white Ford 250 skidded into the yard from the east. Dust that the van raised slanted to the east before the wind and combined with the truck's plume.

The pickup driver was a lanky man. His beige cowboy hat had sweat stains above its brim, and his boots were coated with mud. He walked toward the concrete blocks where the girl stood.

"Apa," the girl said, greeting the man.

"Teresita," the man said. He put his hand on her neck so that his thumb stroked her jaw as a kind of embrace. He nodded toward where the van had last been, on the curve in the road. “Who’s that?” he asked the girl.

Teresita shrugged.

“Why were they here?” he asked.

“They had a sick girl.”

“Why didn’t they take her to Maria Vasconcelos?” the man asked. "She's just a half mile down the road."

Teresita raised her shoulders once more. Sabe solo Dios.

Ways of Seeing

Leonore Hildebrandt

I don't know my neighbor well,
but we've started to walk each other's land—
she cut through the barbed wire fence
and put in a funky gate, tied with shock chord.
From time to time I meet her on the trail.

Last summer, she found a dead mule-deer
in one of the arroyos on my side of the fence.
A mountain lion had come down from the hills.
She got a knife and severed the head from the torso—
to get through the vertebrae wasn't all that difficult.

She carried the head up the slope to a pine tree,
tossed a rope over a high branch,
pulled the thing up by its antlers and tied it off,
balancing it just so. Birds and insects, she hoped,
would work it to the bone.

Instead, it dried up.
The teeth started protruding, the long ears drooped.
That deer's head hangs from its rope, mummified.

The expression is contemplative—it gazes
with half-closed eyes toward the desert.
On my evening walk, I sometimes look at it.
And sometimes I don't.

The rest of the carcass was dragged off,
scattered by hungry jaws. Gradually it vanished–
–
only bits of fur remain in the gully.

Last week, on a hike in the forest up north,
my neighbor found a cow's head, a skull
perfectly intact, white and clean.
She carried it out—three miles.
It was heavy.

At home, she colored the bone with bright,
emphatic swirls.
In the eye sockets, she fastened small bouquets
of dried flowers.
Now the cow peers through a flowery lace
into an Italian lady's living room. I wonder—
can my neighbor be known by way of blossoms?

Charlie Wade

John Little

The Eastern sky was barely starting to glow when Charlie Wade walked into Ruby's Café and took a seat at the counter.

"Coffee please. Black."

"One black coffee coming up." said the waitress. "Will you be eating? The cook won't be here for another 30 minutes but there's a few donuts from yesterday. You here for the bus? It's the Greyhound stop next door that keeps us in business."

"Yes Ma'am, I'm here for the bus. No donuts, thank you. You look like you might be Ruby's daughter?"

"Yes, Ruby was my mother. I'm Rachel. Did you know her? She passed away last year."

"I'm really sorry to hear that. Yes, I knew her. As well as you can know someone you only see for a weekend or two. I used to pass through here on my swing through West Texas to play at Bucky's Bar, but that was a while back."

"More than a while. Bucky's closed 30 years ago when the freeway passed us by. That and the oil crash. Bucky's quit a few years after the drilling crews left."

"Has it been that long? Where does the time go, Rachel? By the way, I'm Charlie Wade."

"Well, that name rings a bell. You're the country singer she talked about. She sounded like it was more than just a casual friendship."

Charlie spun a quarter turn left on the counter stool to stare out the window at the fading stars before mumbling, "You're right. It was more than casual. One night we talked at Bucky's after closing time and I gave her a ride home. She told me her husband had a severe head injury and needed constant care. She felt trapped but made it clear she wouldn't leave him. I left the next day for my next job and never saw her again."

"So where are you off to now? I don't see a guitar and your bag is barely large enough to hold a change of clothes. I've seen enough Greyhound riders to tell you're not a regular."

"You're right, Rachel. See these hands?" he said holding up misshapen fingers. "I can't play anymore so I sold the guitar for bus fare. My sister said she had an extra room for me and that's where I'm headed, back to Abilene where I started. What's in my bag is all I own."

"Good Lord. That's all you own after a lifetime?"

"That's my story. It must sound pathetic to you, but it was the life I chose. Driving from town to town and playing in bars isn't for everyone, but it fit me. I can't explain it. Tell me about your mother."

"Well, my father was no angel. And then when the oil drilling stopped, he lost everything and became despondent. He started drinking and one night crashed his car at high speed. The deputy said it was probably a failed suicide attempt. It left him nearly brain dead, but he lived another 10 years. Since I was born two years after his injury, I figured he couldn't be my real father.

"Good Lord, how'd that make you feel?"

"Confused. I heard he had mistreated my mother, but not from her. She took care of him till the end and, apparently, went to Bucky's a few times before it closed."

"So why didn't she leave this town with you after he died?"

"I used to think it was because this is where she was born and raised, but now I'm not so sure. She used the insurance money to start Ruby's even though she knew the town was dying. From what you're saying, maybe she was waiting for you to outgrow your road music and settle down. After all, Abilene's not that far away."

"You make it sound like she was waiting for me all that time. Why would she do that?"

"That's a good question. Wait here, I have something to give you." Rachel walked into the kitchen and returned with a sealed envelope with the name 'Charlie Wade' scrawled on it. "She left this for you in case you came back."

Charlie opened the envelope and took out a photo of a little girl sitting on a blue tricycle. On the back was written, "May 10, 1973". Bewildered, he passed the photo to Rachel.

"This must be me on my 3rd birthday. The tricycle was my present."

At that moment the cook arrived, interrupting their conversation. "Morning, Rachel, the bus is here. I'll light the grill."

Standing, Rachel said, “I’ve got work to do; want some breakfast?” Then, putting her hand on Charlie’s arm, whispered, “I think we have some serious things to talk about. Please stay a while, I’ve got an empty room too.”

Prayers

William Lloyd

Two men with full hearts
Both bent knee to pray
'Twas in the very same land
On the very same day

One knelt amongst peers
To the side of a throne
One knelt in the woods
He had gone there alone

One called loudly to god
In a manner quite grand
One place hand on the earth
And gave thanks to the land

One listed each treasure
That he'd managed to hoard
And naming each loudly
Gave thanks to his Lord

One sprinkled cornmeal
Before him on the earth
And thanked powers that be
For his new baby's birth

One asked for power

To influence and impress
To increase his yield
And make expenditures less

One asked for knowledge
Of where certain herbs grow
That he may harvest use them
To even life's flow

Two men and two prayers
In their own way each was rich
One was a Christian
One was a witch

Won Wishes Come True

Shanon Muehlhausen & Emily Egge

Flyn pretends he doesn't notice the women and their glares and disapproving noises. He's been doing it his whole life. He runs past them.

"There's Bobber." He sees the bright-red hair of Nemesis #2 and increases his pace.

The day is hot; it always is on Race Day, but it doesn't thwart the crowds. Hundreds of lawn-chaired watchers cheer or jeer the athletes from the sidelines.

"Two miles left," an announcer declares, as the course zigs around yet another castle.

"That castle's the first wish I remember," Flynn thinks. That was ten years ago; there had been a lot of wishes since then.

The next group of women he passes are conspicuous with their hostility. It's hard not to look. They are even more beautiful when they're angry. And they are always angry.

"Damn these leather pants," he thinks.

Leather pants had been three very, very long years ago. The idiot who won the race had been unprepared. He crossed the finish line, gasping and barely able to stand. But like all winners, he had to make his wish immediately.

"I wish we could all wear leather pants, all the time!"

Now, everyone pays the price. Women and men alike, skinny and obese, elderly and infirm, all wear leather pants. The babies are the worst, though. There is something just not right about an infant in leather pants.

Bobber looks over his shoulder and spots Flyn making his move.

"I want this!" Bobber growls through his teeth.

It's true, and Flyn knows it.

Bobber is stupid and primal; whatever he wishes for will be violent or absurd. Flyn flies past him.

"One down; one to go."

By the time Flyn was born, most of the big wishes had already been wished. There was no more poverty, war, terminal illness or advertising. The town actually had more colleges than castles. Of course, countless men had wished for beautiful women. These women just materialized, full-grown, with no memories or families or coping skills. Yeah, they were angry.

Some years, wishes were inspired by a prior wish. “Everyone will drive a sports car” went well with “no one will ever lose their keys again!”

Then there was the regrettable wish that dragons were real, followed the next year by the inevitable extinction of dragons.

These days, the wishes were more personal. All orange juice tasted fresh-squeezed and the air smelled like Tony’s grandmother’s spaghetti sauce.

People spent all year preparing for the race, either training or making deals with people who were training. It was a town of wishers, not workers.

Flyn scans for Kariq, ignoring the throb building in his chest.

Nemesis #1 is going to be hard to beat. The tallest, strongest, and cockiest man in town, Kariq had won last year. Everyone knew what he would wish for if he won again.

“The winners are not all bad; think of your father.”

He ignores his mother’s voice in his head and the pain in his side. His father was known as the village idiot, the only one to have ever wasted his wish. Only

Flyn could make that wish worthwhile.

He is at the center of town now -- a plaza marked by a 600-foot gold-framed portrait of Elvis.

“One mile to go!” The announcer booms.

His lungs and muscles burn, beg him to slow. But he spots Kariq -- and gives his last push.

He knows he doesn’t have much left in him, which makes the footsteps behind him all the more painful. Knowing that turning around is a mistake, he does so.

It isn’t Bobber; it’s two women. They both look like Barbie, and they’re passing him.

Flyn can’t beat them; his knees wobble and he forces himself to slow.

Ahead, Kariq hears the women approaching and accelerates, but he doesn’t look back. He focuses on the prize.

Flyn watches as the women gain on the leader, the determination in their stride fueled by pure hatred.

“They’re not gonna let him wish for more women,” Flyn thinks. “They’re going to win.”

But he was only partially right.

At the last second, the women hurl themselves at Kariq's legs, tripping and attacking him in a cloud of leather-clad limbs and dust.

Flyn can't react quickly enough. He stumbles over an arm and sprawls forward.

As he falls, time slows. He had wanted to win and he hadn't wished for it, he had worked. This wasn't supposed to end with a mouthful of mud.

He lifts his head, smears the dirt from his eyes, and suddenly someone's there, shoving something toward his lips -- he hopes it's water.

A voice in the crowd yells, "Maybe he'll wish for a baby, like his dad," and the audience erupts in jeers.

"Congratulations. You have won the race. You must wish immediately."

Flyn pushes himself to sitting and that's when he sees the bright red of the finish line under his hand, and the microphone shoved hard against his face.

"Immediately."

"I wish that everyone could make their own wishes come true."

--

One year later, it's Race Day again.

A horn blows and Flyn joins the massive crowd at the start. The shot fires and they're off.

When the dust clears, all that's left are people too old to run and several dozen babies in leather pants, lolling in the dirt.

What Flyn had meant by his wish was that if you tried, if you cared, your wishes could come true without winning a race.

But what the town took from it was that EVERYONE should race.

And now Flyn had to win again.

This year, his wish was realistic, not at all confusing, and would benefit everyone. He had to win. He had to do it.

He had to wish away the leather pants.

Reading Blood

by Serene Vannoy

"We are linked by blood, and blood is memory without language." Joyce Carol Oates

That spring morning, they wouldn't let my mother go near the 7-Eleven because they said the blood on the floor would have upset her too much.

It was my blood.

My lifeblood was pooled there, static, lifeless, crimson Rorschach on well-lit linoleum, liberated from my body by a blade I never saw coming.

It had been an uneventful night at the 7-Eleven. I wasn't supposed to come out from behind the counter while working the graveyard shift alone. It wasn't safe. Then again, we gravers were supposed to have a list of chores done by the time the owner came in at 6: floors swept, impossibly preserved foodstuffs in plastic bags tidied, impossibly preserved rolling hot dogs placed on their rollers, coffee made.

Making coffee in one of those big, convenience-store pots is a mindless, dead-easy task. I have muscle memory of the task. I did it every night for months. And then the next thing I remember, I was trying to figure out what was grabbing me, what was wrapping danger around me.

I know nothing about what happened between 2:45

a.m., when my brother left -- he had stopped by to visit me and play video games before going home to bed -- and 3:00 or so, when the attacker came into the store. I probably had the radio on; I sometimes think so. Maybe I was singing to myself, as I usually do when I get tired. This convenience-store gig was an easy way to get extra money, and it was two blocks from my house, where while I sold beer and nachos and tampons and motor oil, my mother slept and my brothers watched late-night TV. I thought the money was worth a few hours in harsh fluorescent lighting with a sign that said, "These premises are under video surveillance," even though the owner was too cheap to buy an actual camera.

#

Blood type is a fascinating thing. Those letters -- A, B, AB, O -- are descriptions of what your immune system is doing at a cellular level, what your cells will fight, what they will kill or be killed by. Sometimes a pregnant woman's body reads her unborn child's blood as a sign of alien invasion, and her immune system will send cells into the baby's blood cells to rupture them from the inside out. Her own baby becomes unsafe because of the signals its blood sends to her. Her own baby.

#

My brother left to go home to our mother's house, to be safe with her, to spend his last night innocently believing we would keep each other safe. The attacker came in around fifteen minutes later. When he came into the store, I must have said hello, but even the next day, I couldn't remember doing so. Almost thirty years later, there is still so much I don't know about that night. I looked it up: the high temperature that day was 90; the average was 72 -- another perfect day in San Diego. But there's so much I don't know: Did I talk to him before he walked behind me -- I must have presumed it was to look in the milk case -- then silently reached around me to stab me in the abdomen? Did he say hello back to me? Did he drive there himself, impaired as he was, or was there someone waiting in the truck to drive him home from this macabre errand?

My blood was sticky between us as he showed me what I saved my virginity for. I don't know how much blood it was. All they would ever tell me was "a lot."

I know that I'm supposed to be upset when I tell you that he raped me. Maybe more upset than when I talk about his trying to kill me. I can't count the number of people who have told me they would rather die than live through being raped. I was twenty-three. I'm fifty now. I won't tell you how to feel, but personally, I cannot conceive of wishing that that terrifying night, lying on a rubber mat on a linoleum floor, covered with a dusting of sticky coffee grounds, and being kissed with rubbery, whiskey-smelling, pasty-pink lips, would be the very last thing that would ever happen to me. During most of the attack, he seemed nearly catatonic. He spoke barely a word. He stared someplace in the vicinity of my left ear when he wasn't kissing me. I got the distinct impression that he was not really present.

#

Blood dies quickly after leaving the body, after hitting the air. Even donor blood, refrigerated, handled with care, doesn't last forever. Stiffens in a couple weeks, gets tossed in six. Becomes useless. At its best, kept in the body, safe in the closed system, blood has maybe a hundred days to live. Is always on death row.

#

Suddenly, a change came over him. His eyes widened, his whole countenance stiffened in terror. He looked as I imagine I would look if I suddenly awoke in the 7-Eleven, raping someone I'd just stabbed. I'm not excusing him, but in that moment, I had compassion for him. The moment didn't last long, though, because then he decided to kill me.

He raised his arm, still holding that damn hunting knife whose mere saw-tooth outline will give me a shudder no matter where I see it for the rest of my life, and prepared to stab me to death. Until then, I'd been compliant, so he wasn't prepared for the fight I put up. I'm surprised now that I had enough blood in my system to fuel the muscles I needed to fight for my life. I kicked and screamed and kicked some more, until finally he told me to stop screaming. My cells were being stained red by the same air that carried my cries and pleas to no one's ears. My mother slept peacefully, two-tenths of a mile away. She will never forgive herself. She says I am in her blood. He paused over me, breathing booze into the air between us, looking like he had no idea how to manage this situation. Neither did I, but I begged, and pleaded, and wheedled, and offered him money or beer or whatever he wanted. I said I would never tell. I said if I ever breathed a word, he could come and kill me.

He quietly consented. He let me talk him into taking some money from the till; I tried to manipulate him into touching the cash-register keys so he'd leave fingerprints, but no dice. And then he left the store.

I never saw him again.

#

"Of all that is written, I love only what a person has written with his blood." -- Friedrich Nietzsche

#

Long minutes later, I told the 9-1-1 operator, a Southern woman who seemed unruffled by my panic, that I was embarrassed because I wasn't wearing underwear.

By the time the ambulance arrived, I've been told I was very nearly dead. Exsanguination. I wasn't having much success getting my blood to stay where it belonged, though I pressed hard with flattened palms, not noticing until later that my thumb was nearly severed from a defensive wound.

The ambulance driver wondered aloud why I hadn't been life-flighted. The EMT asked him if he could go any faster. I was afraid to ask if this meant I was going to die. I don't know how much blood they poured into me on that ride, but it wasn't so much dripping as pouring from the bottom of the slack plastic bag on the hook into the tube they'd inserted -- where? my arm? my chest? I forget. I remember that blood, though. It reminded me of raspberry sauce being piped onto a dessert plate from a squeeze bottle, and I was just lucid enough to find that thought wildly inappropriate and amusing. I began to shake with the chill of shock. The tube of blood connecting me to the bag seemed hot in comparison on my arm.

#

Hot blood is passion. It's anger, too. It's what makes your cheeks flush and turn warm when you see something you're not supposed to. Or when the paramedics cut off your pants and expose your nakedness. Or when the trauma surgeon tells you you'll probably die on the table because you're so obese. Or when the next doctor tells you you're lucky you're so big, or else the knife would have cut your spinal cord. Or when they ask you and ask you and ask you if you knew him. As if somehow someone knowing someone could excuse or explain why he left her blood on the floor of the 7-Eleven.

#

Anger is healthy. Anger is the impetus for putting things right, sometimes. Anger makes a twenty-five-year-old woman decide she's not going to sleep with the light on any more, because that prick isn't going to have that kind of power over her any more. Anger turns her into a poet who spills poems like blood, fearless, having already cheated death. Who is she going to be afraid of? A poetry slam audience? Don't make me laugh.

The blood preoccupies me, I don't mind admitting. I wanted to see it before they cleaned it up. I wanted to know how much there was. I wanted to know -- I *want* to know -- what kind of person cuts first and rapes later, rather than the other way around. I think about requesting my medical chart so I can see how many pints they transfused into me.

And always, always, I think about my mother, trying to reach my side, and being told No, you can’t go near your daughter. Her blood isn't safe for you. It will attack you, consume you, burst your cells from the inside.

Thrift Store Justice

Kit West

After two years of drought the monsoon had finally arrived, arrived like a blessing, yes, but also like a nightmare of being pressed to the ground and held there by an invisible force. The clouds were white, tall and puffy, then, condensed by the force, became black and low and alive with horizontal lightning.

Inside The Perfect Fit thrift store, I watched the storm lower. I also watched a tall Hispanic man try to fit a newly purchased cabinet into his small, black car. He was having a hard time. The woman behind the counter glanced out the window too, following my gaze.

"Oh, no!" She exclaimed.

"What?" I asked.

"I don't think he paid for that!" She answered, charging for the door, jaw clenched.

As I continued watching, the storm clouds lowered even more, until they hovered right above the man's head. I looked at him again, more closely this time. Hispanic, yes, around the eyes, but with a Buffalo Soldier coffee tint and hair that surrounded his face like a shadowy halo. There was also a tribal quiet in his features, a measured quality to his movements, a stillness, as if life were a dance he knew well, as if he were ancient when in fact he was quite young.

The storm broke, releasing a bolt of lightning that struck the unwieldy cabinet, which turned to ash in the man's hands. By this time the woman was upon him, shouting and waving her thin, pale arms. It began to rain, going from nothing to pouring in seconds. The man's brown t-shirt stuck to his chest, giving him a sculpted look, a bronze statue of an ancient hero, or a saint. He blinked and wiped his face with blackened hands, leaving smears across his cheeks, like warpaint.

But this was no fighter; he only stood a little taller while the woman, perfectly dry, continued her tirade, unaware of the storm they shared.

brevity is not my strong suit

Melanie Zipin

brevity is not my strong suit
I prefer free flowing dresses
slowing my steps
dragging my feet
against the sun-warmed earth

they are toughening up –
my feet
sometimes stepping on *goatheads*
or prickly grasses
sharpened rocks
sometimes, luckily, on sandy dirt
or oak and pine needles
mulched by time
—it is the desert
but it's high
most people don't understand that

and they lead me round
and round –
my feet
until I'm dizzy

laying on the ground
bone to rock
digging my spine
into my spot
working down my troubles –
arms and feet
spread wide, stretched long

my eyes wander

up,
I wish I was there
floating with the clouds
meeting all the makers

then down,
bits of earth
slipping through my cupped hands
fierce flora growing everywhere
through this resilient land

then, side to side
my body looks strange
trying to sprout sideways
like some invasive grasses
on a jagged cliff

from my peripheral vision
I can see
dangling earrings
bouncing rainbows
off the side of my nose
which is like a magic sphere –
my peripheral vision
appearing only when…
and then, on to

lost causes
deep breaths
hints of jasmine
4'oclocks and
mimosa blossoms
waiting for rain
birds of paradise

contemplating
flights of redemption
long-suffering thirst
turned to full moon dances
and wicken laughter
casting spells
of love
softening the hardened ground
with tears,
simple joys
surface pleasures
running deep
into my veins

Cross My Heart
Lynne Zotalis

New Mexico has a heartbreaking practice of consecrating their inordinate amount of traffic deaths depicted in the following poem:

Across this state
I'm counting crosses
12, 13, stories buried, 14, 15,
memorializing someone's life and death
to help us remember, ponder, relate to the loss, 16,
"my son is late," mother says, "dinner will wait,"
17, 18, 19, 20, too, too many gathered
with plastic piles and white Styrofoam bits,
pop bottles, beer cans, cardboard boxes at rest
where you died
21, "it can't be," she murmurs to the uniformed
harbinger
at the door, uttered phrase, "we regret to inform"
collapsed in shock, can hear no other sound
22, 23, 24, and 3 more makes 27 if there's a
heaven, I hope they are there
What if I stopped to say a prayer?
28, 29, 30, now a green fender, car case, billowing
WalMart sack clings to cat claw
over dilapidated sofa, an orange pail, would it
help
if I paid tribute?
31, 32, you were loved by someone, maybe many
a daughter, grandson, spouse, best friend

now making a fresh make-shift grave
highway workers respect what we'll never forget,
spangled, glittery, gloriously gaudy
33, 34 trying to reflect the light they were in our eyes—
theirs forever shuttered with black.
5 in a row was the worst I observed.
Carnage.
Autocide.
Curly shredded tire cords
carrying semis laded with our necessities,
maybe that blow-out planted a cross,
shattered the thread of life,
inscribed, all caps [M-I-S-S-I-N-G] under a flag
of blue jeans draped on spindling shrub.
35, 36 two spirits woven as one; a young woman's
smiling face could not escape
the appointment.
71 on this route today…
I'm counting crosses
across this state.

Writer Bios

Ralph Bakshi is an animator, filmmaker, writer, and painter. He has directed nine theatrically released feature films, five of which he wrote. He has also been involved in numerous television projects as director, writer, producer, and animator. Info about his current artwork and projects can be found at ralphbakshi.com

Shelly "Badassia" Barnett moved to New Mexico, seeking warmth and sunshine after life in the Pacific Northwest. A lover of trees—Poet-trees, Creativi-trees, peach and magnolias, her life is good. She reinvented her poetic style when she moved to Albuquerque in 2018. Falling in love with Open Mic and Spoken Word, she often dances the line of both when performing. She became a seasoned resident of Silver City in 2022. Mother, activist, teacher, artist and poet, she speaks her truth, even if her voice shakes. "Magnolia Memory" is her first published piece in a book project.

Claire Rose Byer loves Silver City. An avid traveler who thinks life is for learning, she now works at WNMU and hosts Peep Show, Monday nights at 9PM on KURU 89.1FM.

Xavi Beltrán is a Latin-American writer who spends most of the year in Silver City. Inspired by New World history and geography, and the Magic Realism of authors like Borges, Isabel Allende, and Garcia-Marquez — Beltrán is a two-time recipient of the Bowdoin Prize, the oldest literary award in the United States. Beltrán writes with a strong sense of purpose and place, often about family histories; transgenerational narratives or trauma; homelands and immigration; and the endlessly fascinating strangeness of everyday life. Professionally, Beltrán assists many Grant County nonprofits, and has a rambunctious pet goat named Fuego.

Erica Ciaglia likes to name her cars. Currently she has a hatchback named Mischa, though once she had a Volvo sedan named Al Capone because it had a two-body trunk. This July marks her third year in Silver City.

Natalee Drissell lives in Silver City, New Mexico year round, and attends WNMU as a Visual Art Major and English Minor. She likes to say she's pursuing a degree in storytelling. When Natalee is not hiking the Gila Wilderness, or performing in local theater productions, chances are she can be found writing anything from non-fiction to poetry. She also is a lizard enthusiast (much to the local lizards' chagrin).

Emily Egge likes hanging out with her reader friends- talking about books, talking about writers. There is always another writer for her to fall in love with, thanks to them. When it comes to writing- she prefers to do that with her reader friends too. She has lived in Silver CIty (on and off) for a long time.

Savvy Egge: I am a local musician and songwriter. I enjoy playing music for people. I am 15 years old and attend Aldo Leopold Charter School. I appreciate any opportunity to contribute my art to the community.

Gabe Eyrich holds an MAIS degree in Creative Writing and Psychology. She lives and works in Silver City, New Mexico where she explores the narratives alive in both inner and outer landscapes. Concerned with the nature of soul and psyche, she writes from lived experiences to communicate, connect, and understand. www.gabeeyrich.com

Dawn Falch: I grew up in the midwest but crossed the Mississippi in 1984 and have never looked over my shoulder once! A relative newcomer to Silver City, I nurture my creative self, care for my spiritual self and show gratitude for my physical self by staying active and eating well. My current goals revolve around my yoga & mindfulness practices and the beginnings of a book about my grief journey, after losing my beloved husband in a tragic accident in late 2020. I have three grown children, 3 grandcats and 2 granddogs.

Feral Farm Girl is the pen name of Steffanie Mininger-wife, homeschool mother, and animal rights advocate. She spends her days caring for her family, garden, hobby farm, helping in her father's 300 acre pecan orchard, and managing her 501(c)3 cat rescue/sanctuary, The Whimsical Kitty Cottage, where she cares for around one hundred cats of all ages. And in her spare time, or when inspiration strikes, she writes poetry. She lives in Animas, Nm with her husband, five children, seven dogs, and four cats.

Gail Fritz: I live with my husband and 3 small dogs in beautiful Silver City, New Mexico. I enjoy reading, crocheting, sewing, and painting. Writing provides an outlet for expressing hopes, facing fears, and finding contentment in what is.

Tom Hester retired as chief technical editor for the Bureau of Justice Statistics, USDOJ. He has lived in Silver City since 2006.

Leonore Hildebrandt is the author of the poetry collections *The Work at Hand, The Next Unknown,* and *Where You Happen to Be*. Her poems and translations have appeared in the *Cafe Review, Cerise Press,* the *Cimarron Review, Denver Quarterly, The Fiddlehead, Harpur Palate, Poetry Daily, Rhino,* and the *Sugar House Review*, among other journals. She was nominated several times for a Pushcart Prize. Originally from Germany, Leonore divides her time between Harrington, Maine, and Silver City, New Mexico.

John Little: I moved to Silver City, New Mexico in 1991 to teach business classes at Western New Mexico University. After retiring in 2013, I began the creative writing phase in my life; first songs, then poetry, and now short fiction stories. I live with my son 20 miles south of

Silver City in a self-built house on 25 acres. My writing space looks out a large window onto a pollinator garden where I draw inspiration from the hummingbirds, bees, and dragonflies. I find writing stories to be a good way to relive my life, but with some embellishment the second time around.

William Lloyd: Elizabeth and I moved here 11 years ago and bought the original telephone switching station and converted it into our gallery and home. We have operated Lloyd Studios and sold my art for more than 25 years. We are known nationwide for our bone carving and the creation of high-end custom knives and swords and sculpture. We traveled the Renaissance fair circuit for many years, and still run a gallery at the Maryland Renaissance Faire. As well as creating sculpture and art, I have been writing poetry and stories since I was in high school.

If you recognize the name, it's probably because **Shanon Muehlhausen** has taught you math. Also known for having wacky ideas and following them way too far, she has lived in Silver City for 28 years.

Serene Vannoy is a bi poly fat disabled white atheist poet whose best decision in recent memory was moving to Silver City. Her poems have been published in the US and Canada, and she is working on a memoir.

Katherine West lives in Southwest New Mexico, near Silver City. She has written three collections of poetry: *The Bone Train, Scimitar Dreams*, and *Riddle*, as well as one novel, *Lion Tamer*. Her poetry has appeared in journals such as *Writing in a Woman's Voice, Lalitamba, Bombay Gin, New Verse News, Tanka Journal, Splash!, Eucalypt, Writers Resist, Feminine Collective* and *Southwest Word Fiesta*. *New Verse News* nominated her poem "And Then the Sky" for a Pushcart Prize in 2019. In addition, she has had poetry appear as part of art exhibitions at the Light Art Space gallery in Silver City,

NM, the Windsor Museum in Windsor, CO, and the Tombaugh Gallery in Las Cruces, NM. She is also an artist. P.O. Box 2018 Silver City, New Mexico 88062 970-413-1270

Melanie Zipin is a multi-media artist, performer, and writer; composing her musings from the fabric that surrounds her. She has several essays published with *Rebelle Society*, and released her first *Chapbook*, featuring selected drawings and poetry in July 2019. Taking an early departure from her inner-city roots, the New Mexico landscape provides an ideal backdrop for her somewhat obsessive and incessant writing habit. She has one son, and lives with her husband in an undulating house they built from hand-piled mud. https://www.melaniezipin.com

Lynne Zotalis is an award-winning author, poet, and chairperson for the Silver City chapter of NM State Poetry Society. Her short stories and poetry have appeared in *Tuck Magazine, writinginawoman'svoice, The Poetic Bond* and NMSPS anthology *Glissando*, among others. Contributions to anthologies include *Turning Points: Discovering Meaning and Passion in Turbulent Times*, by Changing Times Press. Zotalis'poetry collection, *Mysterious Existence*, published by Human Error Publishing as well as *Saying Goodbye to Chuck* a daily grief journal are available on Amazon. Her memoir, *Hippie at Heart (What I Used to Be, I Still Am)* won a Firebird Book Award and was a finalist in the Best Book Awards.

Upcoming Submission Deadlines

Fall 2023	September 20, 2023
Winter 2024	December 20, 2023
Spring 2024	March 20, 2024

We welcome all written pieces under 3000 words. If your piece is longer than 3000 words, please send the first 1000 words for consideration. Please use the edition you are submitting for in the subject of your email (for example, Fall 2023).
silvercityanthology@gmail.com

Made in the USA
Columbia, SC
14 August 2023

21582467R00052